This book belongs to

Do Princesses Have Best Friends Forever?

By Carmela LaVigna Coyle

Illustrated by
Mike Gordon and Carl Gordon

TAYLOR TRADE PUBLISHING
Lanham · New York · Boulder · Toronto · Plymouth, UK

Warning: Detachable parts.
Not for children under 3 years.

Published by Taylor Trade Publishing
An imprint of The Rowman & Littlefield Publishing Group, Inc.
4501 Forbes Boulevard, Suite 200, Lanham, Maryland 20706
http://www.rlpgtrade.com

Estover Road, Plymouth PL6 7PY, United Kingdom

Distributed by National Book Network

British Library Cataloguing in Publication Information Available
Library of Congress Cataloging-in-Publication Data Available
978-1-58979-542-6 (cloth)
978-1-58979-543-3 (electronic)

♾™ The paper used in this publication meets the minimum requirements of
American National Standard for Information Sciences—Permanence of Paper
for Printed Library Materials, ANSI/NISO Z39.48-1992.

Manufactured by Friesens Corporation
Manufactured in Altona, MB, Canada in April 2011
Job #64344

To my friends near and far . . .
who pick up right where they leave off.
— clvc

Mommy, can my new friend come over to play?

Why don't you see if she'll stay the whole day!

Are you a princess just like me?

I've been a princess since I was three!

Let's play dress up in
my mom's fancy gowns.

Now all we need are two daisy crowns.

Do princesses make forts with blankets and sheets?

That's where we'll share our deee-licious treats.

Whoops! We dropped crumbs all over the room!

Here comes Mommy to hand us a broom.

Princess, let's stomp in the mud with bare toes.

And then we can rinse them off with the hose!

Do princesses sing on the way to the zoo?

Yes! Maybe my mom will sing along, too.

How do zookeepers pick up the poop?

The zoo must own a very big scoop.

Do princesses swing from limb to limb?

We'll act like monkeys on the jungle gym!

Mommy, can we stop at the ice cream shop?

Oh, *pretty-please-with-a-cherry-on-top!*

Can princesses play in a musical band?

Our neighbors will think we're the best in the land.

What if a princess makes someone feel sad?

Then it's her job to say, "Sorry, my bad."

Let's make two bracelets with a double pink heart.

And then we can wear them
when we're apart.

I wish our playdate would never, ever end.

That's how it feels to have a best friend.

Princess Friends Forever